Dear Parents,

 This is a Stepping Stone Book™ by the Berenstains. We have drawn on decades of experience creating books for children to make these books not only easy to read but also exciting, suspenseful, and meaningful enough to be read over and over again. Our chapter books include mysteries, life lessons, action and adventure tales, and laugh-out-loud stories. They are written in short sentences and simple language that will take your youngsters happily past beginning readers and into the exciting world of chapter books they can read all by themselves!

 Happy reading!

The Berenstains

For Francine,
Bear Country's official riding teacher

Copyright © 2002 by Berenstain Enterprises, Inc. All rights reserved under
International and Pan-American Copyright Conventions. Published in the
United States by Random House, Inc., New York, and simultaneously in Canada
by Random House of Canada Limited, Toronto.

www.randomhouse.com/kids
www.berenstainbears.com

Library of Congress Cataloging-in-Publication Data
Berenstain, Stan.
Ride like the wind / The Berenstains.
   p.   cm.
"A Stepping Stone book."
SUMMARY: Sister Bear falls in love with horses and takes riding lessons
on a horse named Old Bess.
ISBN 0-375-81273-3 (trade) — ISBN 0-375-91273-8 (lib. bdg.)
[1. Horses—Fiction.   2. Horsemanship—Fiction.   3. Bears—Fiction.]
I. Berenstain, Jan.   II. Title.
PZ7.B4483 Bffc   2002   [Fic]—dc21   2001047347
Printed in the United States of America   First Edition   June 2002
10 9 8 7 6 5 4 3 2 1

RIDE LIKE THE WIND

The Berenstains

A STEPPING STONE BOOK™

Random House 🏠 New York

When Sister Bear saw Ms. Toni's horses, she fell in love.

Head over spurs.

It was love at first sight.

Sister had seen horses before. There was Farmer Ben's big wagon horse. And they had pony rides at the church fair.

But Ms. Toni's horses were something else. They were tall and slim. They had long, silky manes and tails.

Then Sister saw the sign on Ms. Toni's fence. It said MS. TONI'S RIDING SCHOOL AND STABLE.

Sister knew what she had to do.

She begged to be allowed to take riding lessons.

Mama and Papa thought about it. They saw the light in Sister's eyes. Sister was in heaven when they said yes.

Sister took to riding like a fish to water. She loved the lessons. But they weren't easy. In fact, they were hard. They made her legs hurt. They made her backside hurt.

The first time she was up on a horse, she was scared. It was so high. You could fall off. You could be hurt. You could even break something!

But she didn't fall off. After a while, she began to feel safe.

"Okay, Sister," said Ms. Toni. "I'm going to walk Old Bess around the ring. You just sit easy."

Old Bess was a mare. That is what you call a female horse.

It was Sister's first lesson.

Ms. Toni was holding the reins. She was leading Old Bess around the riding ring.

"How do you feel up there?" asked Ms. Toni.

"Kinda wobbly," said Sister.

"Why are you holding on to the saddle?" asked Ms. Toni.

"So I won't fall off," said Sister.

Ms. Toni laughed.

"You won't fall off," she said. "Just keep your feet in the stirrups." The stirrups were the foot-holders that hung from the saddle.

"Let go of the saddle and take hold of these," said Ms. Toni. She handed the reins to Sister.

Holding the reins made Sister nervous at first.

But after a while, it was fun. There she was, sitting on a giant horse. It was exciting. She felt like the queen of the world. Old Bess kept walking slowly around the riding ring.

Ms. Toni picked up something. What was it?

It looked like a long, thin black snake. It was a whip!

Sister got frightened. "You're not going to whip Old Bess," she said.

Ms. Toni laughed again. "Of course not," she said. "This isn't *that* kind of whip. This is a training whip. I use it to tell a horse what to do. I'm going to tell Old Bess to trot."

Sister knew what a trot was. It was a slow run. She had read a lot of books about horses. That's how she got interested in horses. Now here she was, sitting on top of one about to trot. She was nervous and worried again. It was so high. She kept hold of the reins with one hand. She took hold of the saddle with the other.

"No, Sister," said Ms. Toni. "You must always hold the reins with two hands. That's how Old Bess knows you're in charge."

In charge, thought Sister. *In charge of a giant horse that weighs a zillion pounds. That'll be the day!*

Ms. Toni didn't even touch Old

Bess with the whip. She flicked it in the air. Old Bess started to trot.

Sister went from wobble-wobble to bouncy-bouncy.

Was it ever exciting!

As time went on, Sister learned that there was more to riding than wobble-wobble and bouncy-bouncy.

A *lot* more.

There was mucking out.

That was cleaning the dirty straw and horse mess out of a stall and putting in clean straw. Sister was very good at mucking out.

Ms. Toni told Mama Bear what a good mucker-outer Sister was.

Mama laughed. She was surprised.

"Hmm," said Mama. "She's not so good when it comes to mucking out her *room*."

There was combing the horse's hair with a comb. It got the tangles out of the horse's mane and tail. Sister was very good with the comb.

Ms. Toni told Mama that Sister was good at getting tangles out.

Mama laughed again. "You should hear her when I get *her* tangles out," said Mama.

There was feeding the horse good oats and hay and not too many sweets.

Ms. Toni said Sister was good about that, too.

"Hmm," said Mama. "I just wish I could keep *Sister* away from sweets."

But a funny thing happened. Mama got her wish about Sister and sweets.

Not only that. Sister began taking better care of her room.

And she began getting her own tangles out.

Sister was still Sister. But she had changed.

Everybody saw it.

"It's the horses," said Papa. "It has made Sister more responsible."

Responsible. Papa loved that word. It meant doing what you were supposed to do.

"Yes," said Brother. "She's not such a pain in the neck now. It must be the horses."

"Sister *has* changed," said Mama. "And mostly for the better. But all she ever thinks about is horses. What about school?"

"What about it?" asked Papa.

"Well, just take a look at her right now," said Mama.

Papa looked. Sister was sitting at the dining room table. She was supposed to be doing her home-work.

"Hmm," said Papa. "I see what you mean."

"Sister," said Papa.

There was no answer from Sister. She had that dreamy look on her face again.

"Sister," said Papa.

"Er . . . huh?" said Sister.

"A penny for your thoughts," said Papa.

"I was thinking about tomorrow's riding lesson," said Sister. "It's really going to be something! We're going to have our first jumping lesson—Sally, Jill, Gwen, the whole bunch of us. Not big jumps. Just little ones. I'll be on Old Bess, of course. Sure, she's old. But we're such a great team. . . ."

"Sister," said Papa.

"Yes," said Sister.

"Tomorrow's riding lesson is one thing," he said. "But what about tomorrow's homework?"

Sister sighed. "But school is so boring. As for this homework, it's boring, boring, boring!"

"What *is* your homework?" asked Papa.

"Problems in my numbers workbook, and I have to write a story," grumped Sister.

Papa picked up the numbers workbook. He read the first

problem. "You have seven ducks. You sell three. How many ducks are left?"

Sister threw up her hands.

"Don't know and don't care!" she said. "Who cares about ducks anyway?"

"All right," said Papa. "Let's try it this way. You have seven *horses*. You sell three. How many horses are left?"

"Four, of course," said Sister.

Papa put horses into all the numbers problems. Sister got every one right.

"Now, about this story you have to write," said Papa.

"Boring!" said Sister. "Boring, boring, boring!"

"Oh, I don't know," said Papa. "Perhaps you could write a story about horses."

Sister's eyes lit up.

"Yeah," she said. "A story about horses." She began to write. She wrote a whole story about horses. It was a pretty exciting story. It was about a magical horse. She got an A for it.

But it wasn't nearly as exciting and magical as the adventure that lay ahead.

Ms. Toni's Riding School and Stable had two parts: the school and the stable.

The school was a big, roomy building. Outside, the floor of the riding ring was covered with sawdust. It had a stand where parents sat on show days.

The school had been a barn. The stable had been a chicken house. Ms. Toni's office was in the back.

When Farmer Ben built new ones, he sold the old ones to Ms. Toni.

Ms. Toni made them into Ms. Toni's Riding School and Stable.

She and her groom, Saddle Sam, worked hard to fix the place up.

They put in the riding ring.

They built the stand.

They put in the office.

The hardest part was fixing up the chicken house.

But they did it. They turned it into a good clean stable with ten stalls for ten horses.

Seven of the horses belonged to Ms. Toni. They were an important part of her business. She rented them to weekend riders. The other three horses belonged to Sister's classmates.

Sally had a black horse named Midnight.

Jill had a brown horse named Gravy.

Gwen had a gray horse named Silver.

Old Bess was the oldest and biggest horse in the stable. The other horses trusted her. They often nuzzled and rubbed against her to show their respect. But there was trouble in the stable.

The trouble came from Mid-night.

Sister didn't own a horse. Her classmates were a little snooty about it. Especially Sally.

Sister rode Old Bess. She loved her and took care of her. But it wasn't the same as having her own horse.

Sister's classmates had fancy riding clothes. They were snooty about that, too. Sally was the snootiest.

Sally seemed to have it in for Sister.

Why was that?

Maybe it was because Sister

took such good care of her horse. Sally, Jill, and Gwen didn't always do their chores.

Or maybe it was because Sister was the best rider.

She got the best marks.

She got the best mark for the trot.

She got the best mark for the canter.

She got the best mark for the gallop.

And she was going to go for the best mark in jumping. Not that she wasn't a little scared. Ms. Toni said that was okay. All good riders were a *little* scared.

But there was a problem: Old Bess *was* slow.

She was the slowest horse in the stable.

Ms. Toni had the run of Farmer Ben's woods. She and

Saddle Sam had cleared a racetrack through the woods. It was about a mile long.

Sister and Old Bess lost every race. Sally always came in first. After every race, Sally turned to Sister and

GET A HORSE!

shouted, "Get a horse!" It must have been a joke because everybody laughed. But Sister didn't get it. She *had* a horse. It was Old Bess.

She asked Brother about it at supper. He knew Sally. She was in his class.

He said, "When cars were first invented, they broke down a lot. When people on horses rode past a broken-down car, they shouted, 'Get a horse!' Now do you get it?"

Sister got it. But she didn't like it.

The jumping lesson was about to begin.

Sister, Sally, Jill, and Gwen were in the stand.

Ms. Toni was in the riding ring.

Things were set around the riding ring.

One was a white fence.

One was a big log. It was real wood. But it was hollow.

One was a bit of stone wall. But it wasn't really stone. It was plastic.

"Some folks say horses are stupid," said Ms. Toni. "But they are wrong. It's true that horses aren't smart about reading, spelling, and long division."

That's okay, thought Sister. *I'm not so smart about long division either.*

"But horses are *very* smart about one thing," said Ms. Toni. "They are smart about being horses. They are very good at doing what they like to do."

Sister could understand that. She liked to jump rope. She was good at it. She jumped to a thousand once.

"That's how you train horses," said Ms. Toni. "They love to run. So it's easy to train them to race. It's very hard to get them to do what they don't like to do. Horses don't like to go backward. They hate it. You can train them to do it. But it's very hard."

Sister could understand that, too. Number work wasn't easy for Sister. So she had to work hard to do it.

"Which brings us to jumping," said Ms. Toni. "Sam! Bring in the horses!"

Sam came in the big open door. He was riding Old Bess and leading

Midnight, Gravy, and Silver.

Midnight tried to pull away from the other horses. Then he bumped against Old Bess.

"My horse doesn't like being led," said snooty Sally. "And he doesn't like that bossy Old Bess either."

Saddle Sam snapped the reins against Midnight's nose. Not hard, but hard enough to make him stop bumping Old Bess.

Sally leaped up.

"Don't you *dare* hit my horse!" she shouted.

"Please sit down, Sally," said Ms. Toni. "You should teach your horse better manners."

"He's just frisky," said Sally.

"Yes," said Ms. Toni. "But where does *frisky* stop and *mean* begin?"

Sister didn't say anything. But she smiled inside.

"All right now," said Ms. Toni. "Another thing horses like to do is jump. Some horses are better at it than others. But they all can do it. What we're going to do is jump over the fence, the log, and the wall. They're far enough apart to get up speed. Here's what you do. Bring your horse to a canter. When you come to the jump, crouch down a little. Then as your horse jumps, you lean forward. The horse will do the rest. Sally, you're first. Mount up and let's see what you can do."

But Sally didn't put Midnight into a canter.

She put him into a gallop.

That was too fast.

Midnight knocked over all the jumps.

"Set them up again, Sam," said Ms. Toni. She turned to Sally. "We know how fast Midnight is, Sally."

Do we ever, thought Sister.

"But jumping isn't about fast,"
said Ms. Toni. "Do it again, Sally,
only this time at a canter."

Sally put Midnight into a canter.
They cleared all the jumps.

Now it was Jill's turn. She and

Gravy cleared all the jumps, too.

Gwen was next. She and Silver cleared the white fence and log with room to spare. But when they came to the wall, Silver stopped short. Gwen was almost thrown off. She was shaken up. It could have been a bad fall.

Ms. Toni took the reins. She patted Silver on the neck.

"It's okay, Gwen," said Ms. Toni. "Your horse may have had trouble with a wall once. But not to worry. You just never know with horses. And that's what makes horses so interesting."

She turned to Sam. "Sam, turn

that jump around. The back doesn't look like stone. Try it again, Gwen."

Gwen put Silver into a canter. They cleared the jump easily.

"All right, Sister," said Ms. Toni. "It's your turn to jump."

"Okay, Bess," said Sister. "Let's go get 'em!"

But what happened next was a little *too* interesting.

Sister put Old Bess into a canter. Midnight snorted and came after Bess.

He reared up and kicked out at her. Old Bess turned and met Midnight's attack. She reared up and kicked back.

It was all so sudden that Sister slipped off. She fell to the sawdust with a thump.

Old Bess was angry. She bit Midnight on the ear. Midnight whinnied and bolted for the open door.

Sister couldn't believe what Ms. Toni did next. She ran after Midnight. She grabbed the saddle and leaped onto Midnight like a trick circus rider. She grabbed the reins from the screaming Sally. She pulled Midnight to a stop.

Sister was still on the ground.

She was shaken up. It had been a pretty bad fall.

"All right," said Ms. Toni. "That's enough excitement for one day. Everybody back to the stable. See to it, Sam. Except for Bess. Tie her to the rail."

Ms. Toni came over to Sister.

Sister's backside hurt.

She was trying not to cry.

Ms. Toni knelt beside her.

"Where does it hurt?" she asked.

"My hip . . . er, my backside really," said Sister.

"Good," said Ms. Toni. "That's the best thing to fall on. It's padded."

Ms. Toni felt Sister's legs.

"Let's see you work your knees," she said.

Sister worked her knees.

"Ms. Toni, why did Midnight go after Old Bess?" asked Sister.

"I think he's jealous," said Ms. Toni. She helped Sister to her feet.

"Jealous?" said Sister. "Why would Midnight be jealous of Old Bess? He can run rings around her."

"True," said Ms. Toni. "But Old Bess is big and powerful. She's the leader of the pack. So Midnight's jealous. Horses are like us. Sometimes they just don't like each other."

Just like Sally doesn't like me, thought Sister.

They went into Ms. Toni's office.

"Sister, how do you feel about riding?" asked Ms. Toni.

There were pictures on the walls.

They showed Ms. Toni riding.

They showed her holding cups and ribbons.

There was one picture showing her standing on a galloping horse.

"Sister?"

"Huh?" said Sister.

"I asked you how you feel about riding," Ms. Toni said again.

"Well, not so good right now,"

said Sister. "Falling off a horse is pretty scary. So I was thinking . . . maybe I should forget about riding for a while."

"That would be up to you, Sister," said Ms. Toni.

It was very quiet in the little office.

"But there's a saying," said Ms. Toni. "When you fall off a horse, you should get right back on."

"There's all kinds of sayings, Ms. Toni," said Sister. She looked at the pictures again. "Did *you* ever fall off a horse?"

"Oh, a couple hundred times,"

said Ms. Toni with a smile. "Come. I want to show you something."

She led Sister to the picture that showed her standing on a galloping horse.

"I used to be a trick circus rider," she said. "I did all the tricks and I took all the falls."

"Ms. Toni!" said Sister. What was this? Who was the horse Ms. Toni was standing on? "That horse looks like Old Bess!"

"It is," said Ms. Toni. "She was *Young* Bess then. We grew up together. I brought her with me from the circus."

"You know something? She

didn't look so sad back then," said Sister. "Ms. Toni?"

"Yes?"

"Why does Old Bess look so sad?" asked Sister.

"Because she *is* sad," said Ms. Toni.

"Is it because she misses the circus?" asked Sister.

"No," said Ms. Toni. "It's because she misses *him*." She pointed to another picture.

It showed Old Bess with a young horse. He was beautiful. He was red. He was the color of fire.

"Bess foaled when I brought her here," said Ms. Toni.

"What's foaled?" asked Sister.

"It means Old Bess had a baby," said Ms. Toni.

"A baby!" said Sister.

"And she's sad because he's gone," said Ms. Toni.

"Did he get sick and die?" asked Sister.

"No," said Ms. Toni. "He got sick of stable life and ran away. He was a mustang."

"What's a mustang?" asked Sister.

"Mustangs are wild horses," explained Ms. Toni. "They don't like saddles or bridles or reins. They don't even like to be ridden. They like to run free."

"Where did he go?" asked Sister.

Ms. Toni pointed to the mountains outside the window. "We think he went there," she said sadly.

"Gee," said Sister. "I'd be sad, too, if I had a baby and he ran away."

"I don't think that's anything you have to worry about," said Ms. Toni. "At least, not for a while. Well, what do you say? Do you want to try those jumps?"

"Sure," said Sister.

Sister and Old Bess cleared the jumps like real pros.

A lot happened that day.

It was a day to remember.

But the thing she remembered most was the fiery red horse that ran away.

Sister had a dream that night.

Ms. Toni was in it. Only she wasn't wearing her riding clothes.

She was wearing tights and a tutu. She sparkled.

She had a long training whip. Only it wasn't black. It was gold.

Snooty Sally was in the dream.

She was wearing fancy riding clothes. They were so fancy they glowed.

Sister was in the dream.

She was wearing rags.

There was going to be a four-mile race. Sister on Old Bess against Sally on Midnight.

It would be a race with jumps. They were like the jumps in the lesson. Only they were much, much bigger.

Ms. Toni held up the training whip. But it stopped being a whip. It turned into a starter's gun.

Bang!

The race was on!

Sally and Midnight were off like a shot.

Sister and Old Bess were off like a snail.

Snooty Sally looked back and laughed.

"Get a horse!" she cried.

It was going to be awful. Sister and Old Bess would lose by a mile.

But something happened.

Something strange.

A thing that can happen only in a dream.

Old Bess turned into her son, the wild horse.

He ran like the wind. He flew over the jumps.

Sister's rags turned into fancy riding clothes.

Sister won the race.

She looked back.

Snooty Sally had knocked over all the jumps. Her clothes had turned into rags. Midnight was no longer a horse. He had turned into a broken-down car.

"Get a horse!" cried Sister in her sleep.

She woke herself up.

Sister knew it was a dream.

She wished it wasn't.

How, oh how, oh how she wished it wasn't.

That snooty Sally! I showed her, thought Sister.

But it was only a dream. The real four-mile race was coming soon. *Then she'll show me.*

Snooty Sally and Midnight would win by a mile. Sister and Old Bess would be dead last.

Sister got out of bed. She went over to the window and looked out.

There was a full moon. It shone on the far mountains.

The next day was a school day.

A regular school day.

Sister was in her regular seat at her regular desk.

But she was a million miles away.

"Sister," said Teacher Jane.

"Huh, er, yes," said Sister.

"It's as if you're a million miles away," said Teacher Jane.

"Er, yes, ma'am," said Sister.

"I do wish you'd pay better

attention," said Teacher Jane.

"Yes, ma'am," said Sister.

The class giggled.

"I asked you to go to the board."

Sister went to the board.

There was an arithmetic problem.

It wasn't a hard problem. It was just some numbers to add up. Sister added them up.

"Correct," said Teacher Jane. "Only I don't like calling on you twice. Please don't let your mind wander again."

More giggles from the class.

Sister went back to her seat. She tried not to let her mind wander.

But it wasn't easy.

She had a lot on her mind.

There was the dream she had last night.

It was lovely. But it was only a dream.

And today was a riding day.

That was good.

But it was also a race day.

That was bad.

Not the four-mile race. That wasn't until the weekend.

The race that was happening today was the mile-long one.

That was bad enough.

Once again, she and Old Bess would come in last.

Dead last.

Once again, snooty Sally and Midnight would lord it over her and Old Bess.

Sister hated it.

Old Bess hated it, too. When they went around the track, Old Bess tried to head off into the woods.

Maybe she should skip riding today. But it would look as if she was chickening out after her fall.

Her backside still hurt a little.

"Sister," said Teacher Jane.

"Er, yes, ma'am," said Sister.

"I don't know what's got into you," said Teacher Jane. "The bell

rang a minute ago and you're still sitting there."

Sister looked around the room. She and Teacher Jane were the only ones there.

It was time to go race.

Sister thought about her dream.

If only dreams came true, she thought.

But they didn't.

Losing to Midnight and snooty Sally was going to be a real nightmare.

Saddle Sam led the riders out of the stable. Sally and Midnight were first in line.

Jill and Gravy were second.

Gwen and Silver were third.

Sister and Old Bess were last—just the way it would be in the race.

Phooey on the race!

Phooey on coming in dead last!

The race began.

Sister knew what would happen.

It would be the same thing that happened the race before.

And the race before that.

Snooty Sally and Midnight would win. She and Old Bess would come in dead last.

What good was being the best rider if you always came in last?

What good was being leader of the pack if you lost every race?

But then something strange happened.

Something that had never happened before.

When Old Bess came to the turn, she left the track.

She went straight ahead.

She crashed through the woods.

What was happening?

Was Old Bess chickening out?

Sister didn't think so.

The woods gave way. They were on a rocky path. It went up. They went up for a long time.

It was as if Bess had been here before. It was as if she knew where she was going.

It was windy.

It was getting cold.

Sister wished she had her windbreaker.

Old Bess twisted and turned as she climbed higher and higher.

Sister looked back. Ms. Toni's Riding School and Stable was far below.

Sister was starting to get a little scared. But she trusted Old Bess. She knew Old Bess wouldn't let anything bad happen. Where were they going?

There were rocks all around.

The air was crisp and clear.

They were in the foothills of the far mountains.

The late afternoon sun was like a fireball in the sky. It was making long shadows.

It was getting late. Sister was beginning to get really worried.

"Hey, Bess," she said. "Where are you taking me?"

Bess stopped.

She raised her head and whinnied.

Her whinny echoed through the mountains.

There was an answering whinny.

It echoed back through the mountains.

The cool mountain air was filled with the echoing cry of horses.

It gave Sister goose bumps.

She looked up.

There on a rocky crest stood the most beautiful horse she had ever seen.

It was the wild horse.

He was almost red. His mane and tail looked like fire in the afternoon sun. He was coming to meet them!

He was even more beautiful up close.

Flame. That's what I'll call him, thought Sister as he galloped toward them.

Flame was glad to see his mother.

She was glad to see him.

They nuzzled.

They rubbed against each other.

He stood side by side with Old Bess.

"Hey, you're squashing my leg," said Sister. She pulled her leg up out of the way.

The mustang wanted Sister to do something.

So did Old Bess.

But what?

Suddenly Sister knew what they wanted her to do. They wanted her to ride him!

But how could she do that?

Flame had no saddle.

Flame had no stirrups.

Flame had no reins.

But he was so fast and so beautiful.

She had to try to ride him.

She slowly slipped off Old Bess.

She slid onto Flame. Off they went.

Sister hugged him with her knees. She leaned forward. She held on to his mane.

He ran like the wind.

What a ride!

What a thrill!

It was almost like flying.

Oh, for a horse like Flame.

Sister looked back. She pretended she saw Sally and Midnight. She pretended it was a big race. She and Flame were winning.

Sister cried, "Get a horse, Sally! Get a horse!"

Her cry echoed through the mountains. "Get a horse! Get a

horse! Get a horse! Get a horse!"

Flame slowed down. He turned around. He trotted back to where Old Bess was waiting. He leaned against Old Bess. It was time to go back. Sister climbed back onto Bess.

Flame and Old Bess said good-bye. They nuzzled. They rubbed against each other.

Sister leaned over and patted Flame on the neck. Flame snorted and whinnied.

Off he went, running like the wind.

"Goodbye, Flame!" called Sister.

Old Bess turned. Back they went. Back down the rocky mountain path.

They met Ms. Toni and the others. They were on their way back from the mile race.

"What happened to you?" asked Ms. Toni.

"Oh, Old Bess and I didn't feel like racing today," said Sister.

But Ms. Toni saw something. She saw that Old Bess's eyes weren't sad anymore.

The day of the four-mile race came.

They would race through the woods.

Saddle Sam led the horses and riders out of the stable.

Sally and Midnight couldn't *wait* for the race to start.

Sister and Old Bess wished the race would never start.

Saddle Sam had tied rags to trees to mark out the course.

They would race to the far side

of the woods and back. The winner would get a silver cup. It was called the Four-Mile Cup.

Sister felt sad as she and Old Bess headed out.

She felt sad for herself. But mostly she felt sad for Old Bess.

Sally and Midnight would surely win.

She and Old Bess would surely come in last.

Ms. Toni was waiting at the starting line.

Moms, dads, sisters, and brothers were there, too.

It was time to line up for the start.

Saddle Sam had a starter's gun.

When they lined up to start, something strange and wonderful happened.

There was a whinny.

The wild horse with the mane and tail like fire trotted out of the woods.

"It's Flame!" shouted Sister.

Everybody gasped.

Flame came over and leaned against Old Bess.

Sister knew what she had to do. She slid over onto Flame.

The starter's gun went off—*bang!*

Gwen's horse, Silver, was fast.

Jill's horse, Gravy, was very fast.

Sally's horse, Midnight, was very, very fast.

But Flame was faster than fast.

Flame was lightning.

Flame was the wind.

Sister held on to his mane.

She squeezed him with her knees.

He flew over the fences.

He sailed over the streams.

He danced over the rocks.

Sister looked back.

Sally and Midnight were far behind.

Jill and Gravy were very far behind.

Gwen and Silver weren't even in sight.

Sister and Flame reached the far turn.

They headed back.

They passed Sally and Midnight on the way.

"Get a horse!" shouted Sister.

The finish was just ahead.

A cheer went up as Sister and Flame crossed the finish line!

Flame nuzzled Old Bess.

Old Bess looked happy.

Ms. Toni looked happy.

Saddle Sam looked happy.

But snooty Sally didn't look happy as she and Midnight crossed the finish line.

She didn't look happy at all.

"No fair! No fair!" she shouted. "Sister didn't ride her own horse."

"Sally's right," said Ms. Toni. "The cup goes to Sally."

But Sister didn't mind. Sister didn't need a cup. She knew who *really* won the race. Everybody knew.

A cheer went up for the real winners.

"Sister and Flame! Sister and Flame! Sister and Flame!"

Flame rubbed against Old Bess. They nuzzled. They whinnied good-bye.

Then Flame trotted back to the wild.

As time went on, Sister became a fine rider. She rode many horses in many shows and many races.

But she would never forget what it was like to *ride like the wind*.

Don't miss the next
Berenstain Bears
Stepping Stone Book™:

TOO SMALL
FOR THE TEAM

HERE IS AN EXCERPT.

Sister hurried to the locker room. She changed and ran out to the field.

There were forty girls on the field. Some kicked soccer balls back and forth. Some practiced dribbling. Some just watched. They *all* were bigger than Sister. Much bigger.

Laura Goodbear was there. She was kicking a ball to big Bertha Bruin.

Sister ran to Coach Brown. "Reporting for tryouts!" she said.

Coach Brown looked down at Sister. Her eyebrows went up.

"Sister Bear?" said the coach. "What are *you* doing here?"

"I just said what," said Sister. "I'm reporting for soccer tryouts."

"I'm sorry, Sister," said the coach. "I can't allow you to try out. You're much too small."

"Small but good," said Sister. "I

can run like the wind. And I'm tricky. I can stop on a dime. I can twist and twirl. And, boy, can I kick!"

"I'm sorry," the coach said. "You're just too small for the team."

Stan and Jan have been writing and illustrating books about the Berenstain Bears for many years. They live on a hillside in Bucks County, Pennsylvania, a place that looks a lot like Bear Country. They see deer, wild turkeys, rabbits, squirrels, and woodchucks through their studio window almost every day—but no bears. The Bears live inside their hearts and minds.

Stan and Jan have two sons. Their names are Michael and Leo. Leo is a writer. Michael is an illustrator. They help their parents write and illustrate the books. Stan and Jan have four grandchildren. One of them can already draw pretty good bears.